OMA

OMA

by Peter Härtling

Illustrated by Jutta Ash
Translated by Anthea Bell

Harper & Row, Publishers
New York, Hagerstown, San Francisco, London

Library of Congress Cataloging in Publication Data
Härtling, Peter, 1933–
    Oma.

    SUMMARY: A young orphaned German boy goes to live
with his grandmother in Munich.
    [1. Grandmothers—Fiction. 2. Old age—Fiction]
I. Ash, Jutta.   II. Title
PZ7.H1195Om 1977   [Fic]   76-58719
ISBN 0-06-022237-9
ISBN 0-06-022238-7 lib. bdg.

Contents

I

How Kalle Came
to Live with Oma

Some people say sixty-seven is old, but Oma didn't agree. Like lots of old people, she always said, "You're as young as you feel." Oma felt pretty young. She also said, "I may be an old woman on the outside, but inside I'm a young girl." Those who knew her well believed her. Oma didn't have much money, and sometimes she grumbled about her tiny pension, or her late husband who hadn't amounted to much either, but she liked laughing better than grumbling. And she knew how to make ends meet. Her apartment in the city of Munich was small, and almost as old as Oma herself. Her sofa had already collapsed several times under heavy guests. The oil stove was the only thing new in the place, and she couldn't really get along with it. She was afraid it would blow them both up someday. Whenever the stove started gurgling she talked to it as if it was a stubborn donkey. She liked talking to herself and her things anyway. That was something you had to get used to when you first met her. Even in the middle of a conversation she sometimes started talking to herself, and if you looked surprised she would simply shake her head, to show it wasn't you she meant.

Everyone called her Oma (which is the German word for grandmother): the people in her apartment house, the baker on the corner, even the boys playing in the courtyard, who sometimes teased her but were fond of her really; they'd even carry her bags up to the sixth floor occasionally. There was no elevator in Oma's apartment house. "Well, we aren't royalty," she would say when she ran out of breath on the fourth floor and had to stop for a rest.

The card on her front door said Frau Erna Bittel in decorative lettering. Her son had once asked her why she put the "Frau" before her name, and she had told him, "Because I want people to call me Frau, stupid! Now that Otto's dead, people might think I'm an old maid. And I'm not!"

Oma's son had a son of his own. This story is about that son and his Oma. His name was Karl-Ernst, but right from the start everyone called him Kalle for short.

Kalle grew up in a small German town near Düsseldorf. His father worked in the office of a factory. He always figured out what the other factory employees should get in their pay envelopes—at least that's what Kalle said.

Sometimes Kalle's father would go to a bar, usually on Friday evenings, and then he'd come home drunk and weep about the world. "Every weekend the same misery!" Kalle's mother would say crossly.

Kalle didn't understand these outbursts, since his father was basically a cheerful man. Kalle got along well with him. Better than with his mother, who was always complaining about the dirt her two men left for her to clean up. She spent the whole day cleaning. Kalle's father said that wasn't normal.

Kalle's parents died in a car crash when he was five. They didn't own a car, had gone for a drive with friends, leaving Kalle with the woman next door. That's where the policeman came; he told the woman, "Both of them are dead."

At first Kalle didn't understand. For a long time he couldn't believe he would never see his parents again. Couldn't believe they were gone for good. "But they can't be!" he kept saying. The woman next door put him to bed, and a doctor gave him a pill, which made him drowsy.

"This will help you sleep. And sleep is what you need, little man," said the doctor.

Kalle thought "little man" was a dumb thing to call him, and he thought the doctor was dumb, too.

9

At the time he thought everyone was dumb because they kept patting him on the head, or hugging him—because they all behaved quite differently from usual.

All except his grandmother. Oma came, and though she cried too, she stopped crying and snapped at everyone, "Life has to go on, and it will go on somehow!" And right there in front of Kalle, surrounded by aunts and uncles he had never seen before, she made up her mind: "I'm taking Kalle, he'll live with me."

"But Erna . . . at your age!" said one of the uncles.

Oma laughed. "Do *you* want him? Tell me! All right then, stop talking nonsense!"

Up to then Kalle had seen Oma only a few times. He had always liked her. She talked a little louder than he was used to, used dirty words, and treated his father as if he was Kalle's age. She called his mother a moaning Minnie and she claimed his father had no backbone. But she called Kalle just Kalle. Never little man, honey, or kid.

She took him seriously.

Kalle was surprised at how quickly an apartment could be straightened up and then emptied. Oma got rid of the furniture. "I don't need all this," she said. Kalle ended up with one suitcase full of his own things, nothing else. With this suitcase, which Oma carried, he left the town where he had lived with his parents. To live with Oma, in Munich.

Now I have the boy! I must be mad . . . an old woman with a child who won't be able to stand on his own feet for at least twelve or thirteen years. Am I supposed to live to be a hundred because of Kalle? But who else in the family would have taken him? They might even have put him in an orphanage. And that wouldn't have been right, no! I bet he'll miss his parents for a long time. Especially his father. But perhaps that's just talk. Lots of children have fathers who might as well not be there at all— I'll pull myself together and refuse to think about being old. Kalle and I, we'll manage.

2

How Oma Is Different

Kalle quickly got used to Oma, though he thought her apartment was pretty funny. But Oma had had her old furniture for years and years; she couldn't refurnish the apartment just because of him. And he *almost* had a room of his own. Oma did her sewing there in the daytime. In the evenings he always had to pick up pins and needles so he wouldn't prick his feet.

Oma was different from other people in many ways. On one of Kalle's first nights in her apartment, he couldn't get to sleep, so he went into the bathroom, which was next to his own room. He got a terrible shock when he saw Oma's teeth in a glass of water. He didn't dare touch them; he was afraid they would snap closed even without Oma.

The next morning he asked, "Since when can people take their teeth out of their mouths? I can't."

"Those aren't my own teeth," Oma explained.

"My teeth are all gone. I've lost them like you lose your baby teeth. Only you don't grow a new set of teeth the third time around, so you get them made."

"Do you have to brush them?" asked Kalle.

But Oma didn't want to talk about her third set of teeth anymore. "It's not that important, Kalle," she said.

The whole day was different at Oma's. Oma got up even earlier than his father used to, though she didn't have any office to go to. She told Kalle why. "I get these sharp little pains all over. It's arthritis."

Kalle had no idea what arthritis was. "You mean someone called Arthritis comes to see you at night?" he asked.

"No, arthritis is an illness old people get," said Oma.

Oma would be rattling around in the room next to his at six in the morning. The sound always woke Kalle up. But since he didn't want to get up so early, he pulled the covers over his head and thought about his father and mother. He did that for many mornings, for several months, until he went to school and made many friends.

Breakfast was at seven. Oma had a cup that was three times as big as the cups at home. She called it her coffee bowl. She filled it to the brim and she slurped. She was doing what his mother had told him not to do.

He said, "Don't slurp, Oma."

Oma looked at him, startled, put her cup down, and said, "Tell me, should you speak to me like that?"

He said, "Mommy always told me not to slurp. And you slurp."

From then on Oma tried not to slurp. She found this so difficult to do that she drank only half of her coffee at breakfast and finished the rest, slurping as usual, after Kalle had gone to play in the other room.

Oma had decided not to send him back to kindergarten, but to keep him home till he was old enough to go to school.

"I think we need these six months to get used to each other, Kalle," she said.

Kalle found this dumb at first, but then he liked it because life with Oma was never dull. In the mornings he helped Oma distribute her leaflets. Oma got the leaflets from factories. They announced a washing-machine demonstration at the Astoria, with free gifts, or told you how you absolutely must buy someone's Superior Coffee Filter.

"It doesn't bring me much money," Oma said, "but it keeps me on the go. Personally I'd never buy the stuff. You have no idea what fools people can be!"

Oma knew people everywhere she went. She always stopped to chat. Kalle thought this was boring, but people often gave him candy, so he said, "I like it when you distribute."

After the leaflets were distributed, it was time to go shopping. The local shopkeepers were scared stiff of Oma, because she was determined not to be cheated. She said, "If I have to turn every penny three times before I spend it, I want to turn anything I buy with it too."

Kalle helped with the turning. This annoyed the shopkeepers. One told him to take his dirty paws off the cucumbers, and Oma snapped, "I bet you don't wash your cucumbers half as often as Kalle here washes his hands!"

Oma had a terrific sense of humor, and Kalle liked that. She was hard to fool, and she wasn't afraid of anyone. Indeed, other people were afraid of her. When she frowned the shopkeepers fell over themselves to be friendly. She was always thinking up new wisecracks. For instance, she would ask the baker, "Been putting your rolls on a diet? They've shrunk some more. And become more expensive!"

Most of the shopkeepers were stuck for an answer. But Kalle came to realize that Oma was poor—poorer than his parents.

"Once I get your orphan's allowance we'll be a little better off," she said. "But the Powers That Be always take their time. They don't think about you and me."

Kalle asked who the Powers That Be were.

"Oh, people who sit behind big desks and push

piles of papers around. They decide who gets money and who doesn't."

Kalle couldn't imagine anyone being that powerful. Sometimes he wished *he* was one of the Powers That Be, so he could give Oma lots of money.

Oma didn't spend as much time cooking dinner as Kalle's mother used to. "Waste of time, slaving over a hot stove," she said.

After meals Oma sat down at her sewing machine, and Kalle could go out to play in the courtyard. At first he didn't know any of the other children there. They laughed at the way he talked. They said he sounded like a foreigner, almost like one of the Turks who come to Germany to work. "I'm not Turkish!" he said, but they wouldn't believe him. When he told Oma, she said, "Why didn't you tell them you were a Turk from the Ruhr district? God, those children are as stupid as their parents! They think Turks are bad just because they're Turks!"

After some time the other children let Kalle play with them. A little later he had his first fight with Ralph, who was seven and ordered everyone else around. He didn't beat Ralph. But he fought so well that Ralph wasn't mad at him.

Ralph had something wrong with him. He talked through his teeth. When he said "s" it sounded like "sh." At first that made Kalle laugh, and he told Oma, but she said, "It's mean to laugh at Ralph.

Most of us have something wrong with us."

"I don't," said Kalle.

"Yes you do," said Oma. "Because you think you don't. *That's* what's wrong with you."

"What about you?" Kalle asked.

"Well, now," said Oma mysteriously. "I have something pretty awful! I'll show you sometime."

A day or so later she came out of the bathroom in her bare feet and pointed to her right foot.

"See that? My little toe is joined to the toe next to it. That's one of the things wrong with me."

"Are there others?" asked Kalle.

"You think I'm going to tell you all of them at once?" said Oma.

Evenings at Oma's were very different from home. Kalle's mother used to bathe him, and sometimes, if it was late, his father would join in and they had a real water battle.

The very first evening, Oma had handed him his washcloth and told him to wash himself.

Kalle had burst into tears, because everything was so strange. Oma had started to cry too, so Kalle had stopped, and started washing himself. That's how it was from then on. Oma always sat on the edge of the tub and watched him while he washed.

"I do believe I can actually see you growing!" she said.

She did dry him, though. She liked doing that. She

rubbed him hard till he was glowing all over, and she always said, "That feels good, Kalle, doesn't it?"

There was one other thing very different from home. When Oma washed herself, she locked the bathroom door. She seemed to be scared of Kalle. After a while he asked her if she was.

"Nonsense, Kalle!" she said. "Old people aren't very nice to look at, that's all!"

"*I* think you're embarrassed to let me see you," he said.

"Quite right, Kalle," said Oma.

He didn't think it *was* quite right, but he couldn't persuade her to leave the bathroom door open.

"You're Kalle," she said, "and I'm Oma. You're young and I'm old. That's the difference. The only one."

Well, it hasn't taken Kalle long to find out things are different here. Dear God, all this progressive child rearing: Am I supposed to run around naked because his parents did? That boy doesn't know what old people look like! And I am embarrassed. I just can't do that sort of thing. I'm old-fashioned. In my day we weren't so—how can I put it?—so shameless! Only shameless isn't the right word. People don't feel ashamed these days, and that's all right too, I suppose. But I can't be like that. He'll just have to understand that.

3

With Oma at
the Welfare Office

One day, when Kalle had been with Oma for over four months and she had put his name down for school, Oma suddenly lost her temper. She had been looking in the mailbox every morning to see if there was any news from the welfare office at long last. The welfare office didn't send anything. Oma's anger grew.

"They do nothing!" she shouted that morning. "They eat their own papers and stick pencils up their noses! I'd like to be a civil servant too!"

Kalle couldn't imagine Oma in an office, but he knew why she was furious. His legal guardian, who had been his father's boss, had filled out forms saying Oma should act as Kalle's foster mother—which, Kalle thought, was all nonsense, since she couldn't really be anything but a foster grandmother. And she'd always been his grandmother. But apparently it made sense to the Children's Welfare people, and the wheels had been set in motion, as they say. Only they didn't move very fast; they went at a snail's pace. And Oma needed official approval of the arrangement so she could get an orphan's allowance for Kalle. And that was very important. After all, Oma was poor and, as she said, Kalle was eating her out of house and home.

Oma decided to "take up the matter with the authorities in person." (She always used very grand words when talking about the Powers That Be.) "You must come too," she said. "You're my proof, Kalle. I want them to have a look at you."

Oma put on her best dress, and she kept on brushing Kalle's clothes. Which annoyed him. Before they started out he ate some rolled oats straight from the package, on purpose, and got himself dusty again.

"You ruin everything!" said Oma. She was in a bad mood.

They took the tram. Oma was silent—not exactly silent, she kept mumbling to herself, rehearsing sentences she had learned by heart for the officials at the welfare office. She took no notice of Kalle.

At the welfare office they were sent to Room 17, and they waited outside for half an hour, sitting on a wooden bench, again without talking. When they finally did get in, the elderly, serious-looking man behind the big desk said no, it was Room 22 they wanted.

Outside Room 22 they waited once more. Kalle could see that Oma was working herself up into a state. She was ready to explode. The man inside Room 22 was pretty young, though he had gray hair—perhaps because he had to care for so many people. He looked at Kalle, then said in a voice like a minister, "So you're the poor little chap!"

Kalle wanted to stick out his tongue, but then he thought it might help Oma more if he acted like a poor little chap, so he looked sad.

Oma plunked herself down on the single chair in front of the desk and said, "Don't get carried away by pity. *Do* something instead!"

Kalle had the feeling that the man was getting ready to run out of the room. But he stayed; he had to stay, that was his job. He asked Oma her name, searched in a file cabinet, and took out a rather fat folder. What a lot had been written about Kalle and Oma! They were famous in the welfare office. Not that it helped any.

The man sat down behind his desk looking very important, licked a finger, leafed through the papers, shook his head, nodded, and said, "It's an intricate matter."

"What's *intricate*?" asked Kalle, who didn't know the word.

"Just what I was wondering myself!" said Oma, answering instead of the man.

"Your case isn't simple," the man said. "You see, it's not really a question of fostering, since you are a relative. The child's grandmother, to be precise."

"You don't say!" said Oma.

"Don't try to be funny, please," said the man.

"I'm not being funny," Oma said. "It's no joke to me, let me tell you! When does the boy get his allowance?"

"Are you dependent on it?" asked the man.

Oma stood up, violently pushing the chair away from her, and said, "Now you listen to me! You *know* what my pension is. It's all written down there. I bet you also know how much a boy like this eats every day, and that he wears out socks and pants, that he needs things! Am I a millionaire? Am I a clothing factory?"

By now Kalle was enjoying his visit to the welfare office. He said, "Oma's right! I do eat a lot. And she's right about my pants too."

"So there!" said Oma.

The man began to laugh. He said, "I'll try to expedite matters."

He really did use some long words.

"You better expedite!" said Oma. "Otherwise I'll be back next week, I promise you!"

The man laughed again and said, "That would be a pleasure! But I'll do what I can to straighten things out."

He shook hands with them both as they left. The moment they were out in the corridor, Oma did a little skip and a little hop (she couldn't hop properly anymore) and said, "What a team we make, Kalle! We'll have to keep it up! No official will be able to resist us."

Kalle thought so too.

I can't imagine being without Kalle now. Sure, he's a bit of a strain, and I'm tired out by evening: That boy really exhausts me. But maybe it's a matter of getting used to him. And he'll grow up, after all.

He often reminds me of his father; makes me feel as if I had a son again. That's silly, of course. I can't treat him like a son, I'm too old. His mother would be better for him, really.

Funny how I still get hot under the collar thinking of her. She wasn't so bad, I suppose. She was a good mother. She did things differently from me, that's all. She didn't keep such a careful eye on the child. Always said they have to learn early to be independent. True enough, but you have to help them learn. Well, she said she did. I didn't think so. It's true, we didn't understand each other. She got on my nerves, and I suppose I got on hers. Now I sometimes wish I hadn't quarreled with her so much.

4

When Oma Tells Stories

Kalle couldn't understand why Oma kept talking about the old days. She wasn't very interested in something that happened yesterday, but she could remember every detail of what happened twenty or forty years ago. She still remembered her first railway journey, and the day she married Grandpa; the dress she wore for her wedding, and what they had to eat. Kalle wasn't very interested.

"It's a help to me, Kalle," Oma tried to explain. "Sometimes the past seems nicer than the present."

That was the difference between Kalle and Oma. Kalle cared only about what was going on that day, what he was doing with his friends, what had just happened to him, what he was planning to do next. Oma did not think these things were important, unless she had to get upset about them. She preferred to get worked up about some of her memories.

"You know, Kalle, I'll never forget how Grandpa

went under that tram and nearly lost his leg, but not quite. He was all covered with blood when they brought him home, and he said, 'I'm not as bad as I look,' and I thought, 'The poor man will bleed to death before my very eyes!' I don't suppose I'll ever get over it!"

She *had* gotten over it, though, long ago. She just found her memories so exciting. If she saw some exciting film on television she'd say, "It's all made up. They can't fool me! You know, Kalle, when our building was bombed out . . ." And off she would go, launched on a story Kalle had heard several times already, except that it was a little different each time.

"Your father had just gone to college when the bombing raids started," Oma said. "No, wait a minute, maybe he was still at school. Those madmen drafted him, right at the end of the war. He was supposed to shoot down bombers. Imagine putting children behind cannons!"

"Great!" Kalle couldn't help saying.

"Great? You think that's great? Just because you kids are always running around with your cap pistols playing war? Let me tell you, children don't enjoy a real war any more than the rest of us—in fact they come off worst. Just think about those poor little things in Vietnam. Where was I?"

"Talking about Daddy," said Kalle.

"That's right. He was still at home, and during the

big raid he sat in the cellar with me. We heard the hum of the bombers coming closer and closer. I was scared stiff. I took the boy in my arms, and a moment later the ground began to shake. Bits of plaster fell from the cellar ceiling. Someone said we must have been hit. And we had been. The building was still standing, but part of the roof was torn away, and our own apartment was in a shambles. And there weren't any windowpanes left. We slept at a friend's house and started to repair the apartment in the daytime. We put cardboard in the windows instead of glass."

Kalle was not listening very hard, because he knew this story already. He was thinking of other things. Like: How could he convince Oma it would be all right for him to play in the courtyard next door, because he got along better with the children there?

Oma wouldn't hear of it. "I have to be able to see you when I look out the window, Kalle," she said. "You're independent enough as it is. Of course I want you to be able to stand on your own two feet, but . . ."

"How do you mean, stand on my own two feet?"

"Well, not clinging to my apron strings forever. But I do have to keep an eye on you."

And then Oma was off on another story of the old days, when there were hardly any cars, and the planes had four wings, sort of double-decker planes: Oma thought those were wonderful.

"You see, they just couldn't crash, Kalle! If one wing fell off, they still had three left."

When Kalle told this to a friend who was older than he was, his friend laughed and said it didn't make any difference how many wings a plane had. "Rockets don't have *any* wings, and they go fastest of all," he said. Kalle told Oma. Oma was horrified. "Rockets only kill people," she said.

Kalle and Oma never really agreed, because Oma preferred to talk about the old days, which Kalle didn't know and which he thought must have been very funny.

Well, the boy ought to know how it used to be! He ought to know how it was when I was young and my name wasn't Erna Bittel but Erna Mauermeister. I wonder why he thinks my stories are boring? He only really listens when I talk about the war, and then he wants to know everything: how you shoot a gun and if there were any dead. There must be some sort of fighting instinct in children. Hideous! Today, when I was telling Kalle how I met Otto, and how I was so excited I got the hiccups and they went on for hours, Kalle just said he'd heard that story already. I know *I never told it before! Ah, well . . . perhaps all this was really too long ago.*

5

Oma Works for Justice and
Kalle Is Embarrassed for Her

Kalle quarreled with Ralph. They had a fight. Ralph tugged at Kalle's pants until they ripped and slid down to his knees. Oma heard the noise in the courtyard. She had already been up and down the stairs to the sixth floor twice—that was really enough for her. But the fight downstairs made her uneasy. She came downstairs. She saw the long rip, Kalle's torn pants, and asked, "Who did that? Who ruined Kalle's best pants?"

She told Kalle, "Didn't I tell you to put on your old pants when you're playing, the ones I mended!

"Who did it?" she repeated.

A few of the children had run away, and those who were left, including Ralph, didn't say anything. Kalle didn't either.

Oma said, "Do you want me to pull your ears, one by one?"

One of the children said, "You can't do that. You'll be punished."

"You could in the old days!" said Oma. "I can do what I want!"

Kalle said, "That's not right, Oma. You *can't* do what you want, and you can't hit children you don't know."

Oma lost her temper. She marched toward the children, who stood watching her.

"You are cowards!" she said.

Kalle came to his friends' defense. "They're not cowards!" he said. "I tore my pants while I was playing, that's all."

"Now you're telling lies too," said Oma. "First a coward, then a liar! Disgraceful!"

Kalle knew that Oma was getting more and more furious. He tried to calm her down. "My pants aren't so bad. If you sew them up again they'll still be good enough for best," he said. "And I'll wear the others for playing, I promise."

"Never mind that now!" said Oma crossly. "It's justice I care about."

Kalle didn't understand. The other children didn't either.

"What do you want?" Kalle asked.

"I want to know who did it."

"And then?" Kalle asked.

"Then I'll tell him what he did wasn't right. And

34

I'll tell his mother she must replace your pants."

"You can't do that!" said Kalle.

"But that's justice," said Oma.

"What if the pants were expensive?" asked Ralph.

"So it was you who tore them," said Oma.

Scared, Kalle assured her it hadn't been Ralph.

Oma got furious all over again. Ralph was about to take off, but she grabbed his arm and shook him, and Kalle shouted, "Don't you hurt him! Just because of justice!"

Oma screamed, "Oh, I could thrash the lot of you, one by one!"

Kalle felt sad and ashamed. That evening he told Oma, "That wasn't right, what you did in the courtyard."

"Why don't *you* mend those pants then," said Oma.

Kalle knew Oma wasn't just concerned about the pants. But how could he have helped her?

All this modern education—I just don't understand it! But I don't want to go wrong either. Oh, they can all go to blazes! If only he didn't run after the dirtiest, loudest, meanest kids around. Street urchins, that's what they are. I know we aren't rolling in money either, but I'd be ashamed to let myself go like that. Kalle doesn't see it that way. He says it's because they don't have a grandmother and that matters and I mustn't blame them for that. Maybe the know-it-all is right.

6

With Oma on Vacation

By now Kalle had been living with his grandmother for three years and going to school for two. He had a lot of friends and couldn't imagine life ever being any different. Sometimes people asked him if it was always good living with Oma. Kalle thought that was a stupid question. He didn't see how it could be any different. Of course they quarreled now and then, but on the whole Kalle thought Oma was great. She didn't complain half as much as the other old women, who came for coffee on Saturdays. They'd start moaning and groaning the moment they came in the door. One had pains in her leg, another got hiccups after every meal, a third complained about her husband. Kalle always made himself scarce, which Oma thought was only fair. She had grown used to the idea of Kalle choosing his own friends. She had stopped giving him advice.

For Kalle's eighth birthday Oma gave him a new

pair of pants and another, very special, present: a vacation for the two of them away from home. Oma said she hadn't had a real vacation for thirty years or more. And the last vacation she could remember, in Tegernsee, had been rained out. Tegernsee is not far from Munich, but it seemed a long way off to Oma, who didn't think the way a driver would. Kalle, who had heard about that last vacation before, was afraid they would be going to Tegernsee again, and he had already been there with his class. He didn't think it was really far enough away to go for a vacation. Other kids at school would talk about Spain and Italy and Holland, even the Baltic Sea. Kalle always said what Oma had told him to say: "*We* had a terrace vacation."

Since he wasn't used to vacations, he didn't need one.

"People are strange," Oma told him. "They go all the way to Spain to go on arguing, and they come home worn out!" Kalle thought that wasn't the whole story, but as usual there was some truth in what Oma said. He remembered his friend Eberhard telling him, "We went to the seaside in Spain, and it was great, only then Mom and Dad quarreled and Mom wouldn't speak to Dad. She didn't start shouting at him again till we were on the way home and he nearly crashed into a truck on the highway."

That wasn't Kalle's idea of a vacation.

On his eighth birthday, Oma gave him a piece of paper which said:

To Kalle (and Oma)
IOU one vacation for two in Furth im Wald
July 14–18
Signed and authorized by Oma

Kalle read the note. He thought it was funny. While he was reading it Oma kept asking, "Well, do you like it? Kalle, what do you say? Well?"

"Where *is* Furth im Wald?" Kalle asked at last. "Is it really in a forest?" In German, Furth im Wald means Furth in the Forest.

"Yes," Oma said, "it's in the Bavarian Forest. It has a railway station, too. That's important, because it means we don't have to go by bus. You remember Fräulein Bloch, who comes here for coffee? Well, she went to Furth im Wald on vacation, and she's found us a place to stay. Somewhere I can just afford. She says the people are real farmers, very nice."

The whole week before, there was no stopping Oma. She kept packing suitcases and unpacking them again. Kalle told her not to be so silly, they didn't need to pack so far ahead, and was sent out of the room. "You don't understand," she said. "I'm not used to traveling anymore."

"But one suitcase is enough," said Kalle. "I don't need to take so many things."

Their train left at six in the morning. Oma got up in the middle of the night. At three she woke Kalle. She was already dressed for the trip. Kalle had never seen her looking like that. She was wearing a suit; its skirt came down almost to her ankles.

"Couldn't you shorten that skirt a little?" he asked.

"But it would be a pity to waste all that good material! Besides, it's fashionable."

She was also wearing a new hat. Maybe it was an old one. In any case, it was a hat she never wore. She mostly wore babushkas. A large pin with a pearl in it was stuck in the hat.

"You might prick people with that pin," said Kalle.

"That's a hatpin," said Oma. "Hats have hatpins, see? Stop finding fault!"

Kalle got dressed. They had coffee and bread and butter standing up, and just before four Oma said, "Time to leave."

"Are the trams running at this hour?" asked Kalle.

"No, we have to walk to the station," said Oma.

"But that suitcase is heavy!" cried Kalle.

"Ha!" said Oma. "My secret weapon's in there!"

She dragged the enormous suitcase downstairs (it had an umbrella and Grandpa's walking stick tied to the top), and when she got to the sidewalk she put it down next to her and drove off with it—there were

40

little wheels fastened to the bottom of the suitcase. They had been Grandpa's too, she said. Kalle suddenly felt everything was great.

They got to the station. It was much too early. Oma had time to look at every platform and read every notice, but she still wasn't really sure their train would leave from Platform 6. She asked five different railwaymen, one after the other. Each gave her the same information. Kalle began to get annoyed, and said, "If you ask one more, I'm running away!"

The train ride was fun. Oma had brought plenty of things to eat, and she shared them with all the other people in their compartment. By the time they changed trains she wasn't so nervous anymore. In Furth im Wald she asked the man in the ticket office how to get to the farmer's house, and whether it was far. "It'll take you two hours on foot," the man told her.

Kalle's heart sank. He was sure Oma would put the heavy suitcase down on the road and march off, on and on for miles. But Oma was a seasoned traveler by now.

"Is there any other way to get there?" she asked.

"There's a bus. Goes direct from the station. If you hurry you'll catch it," said the man.

"What number bus?" asked Oma.

"It's the only bus in front of the station," said the man.

They reached the farmhouse without any more trouble.

The farmer wasn't a real farmer. Though he did have a few cows, he had more rooms than cows, and the rooms were all full of people on vacation.

"Well, every farmer has his cows to milk," Oma used to say later, when she told her friends about the vacation. "They milked us, that's for sure!"

Their room—they had only one—was small, and was under the roof. The toilet was one floor down, which Oma complained about. She said she couldn't go roaming around the house every night like some ghost.

"Then I'd better give you a chamberpot," said the farmer's wife reluctantly.

Kalle thought that was mean of the farmer's wife. Oma did go downstairs every night, grumping and bumping into things and waking everyone up. Kalle was sure she was doing it just to annoy the farmer's wife.

Up to now Oma had always been careful to keep Kalle out of her bedroom. But now they had to sleep in the same room for the first time. This scared Kalle. But Oma arranged it so that Kalle was usually asleep by the time she came up to bed. There was a television in the farmhouse living room, and the guests, Oma among them, sat and watched television every evening. Kalle was sent to bed at least two hours before the end of the evening's programs.

A few times, however, he was still awake when Oma came up, and he heard her getting undressed. It seemed to take her ages. Kalle thought Oma must be wearing four or five dresses, or slips, one on top of the other, because no one would take that long to get undressed otherwise. Once in bed she fell asleep at once and snored. Well, she didn't actually snore, she snuffled. Kalle listened, and then he couldn't fall asleep again.

The following morning, though, Oma would always claim she had hardly slept at all because she had heard Kalle tossing and turning in bed. When he said, "But I was lying quietly on my back for hours and hours!" she'd say, "How do you know? You were sleeping like a log!"

The other guests at the farm were nearly all elderly. There were only two other children in the place. One boy came from Wuppertal; his name was Bernd and he was a year younger than Kalle. The other came from Berlin. He was fourteen and he was bored. Kalle and Bernd went to the stables and the barn together. They thought up lots of games they couldn't play in the city. Kalle liked Bernd. Oma liked him too. But she said his mother was a silly little floozie. Kalle didn't know what floozie meant, but he didn't like to ask. When Oma used words he didn't understand she usually was being mean.

Oma quarreled with their landlady about the coffee they had for breakfast. You couldn't possibly drink it, she said, it was just like dishwater, and it made her feel sick all day. The landlady got terribly angry. No one, she told Oma, had ever said that to her in all her years of having guests, and she had had plenty! No one had ever dared insult her like that! She made very good, strong coffee! Oma laughed sarcastically. Then she said something that really infuriated the farmer's wife. "I bet you stir the boiling water with a cow's tail!" she said. "That's what it tastes like, anyway!"

The farmer's wife told Oma to leave the house at once.

Oma said she wouldn't dream of it—she and her grandson were paying guests.

That's why they stayed. Oma thought the coffee got worse than ever. "It's that woman paying us back," she said.

The one time Oma went on a long excursion with Kalle she fell into a pit dug to store turnips. You couldn't see the pit because it was covered with straw. Oma wouldn't have noticed it anyway, because she was running after a butterfly. Suddenly she disappeared. Kalle heard her shouting from somewhere underground. No, she wasn't shouting, she was wailing. That really worried him. Oma shouting meant

44

things were all right. When she began to wail, something was genuinely wrong.

"Where are you, Oma?" he called.

"You can hear where I am, you fool!" Kalle decided nothing too bad had happened. He went up to the edge of the pit, saw a hole in the middle of the straw, and heard Oma puffing and panting. She was working her way up.

"Can you find a branch?" she said.

"What for?"

"Don't ask stupid questions! To pull me out, of course."

"OK," said Kalle.

He found a long branch, a little worm-eaten, and lowered it into the pit. He could feel it taking Oma's weight. She was very heavy.

"Go on, pull!" she cried.

Kalle pulled, the branch broke, and Oma started wailing once more. She said he was no good for anything. After a silence, he could hear Oma stacking turnips on top of each other.

"What are you doing?" he asked.

"Making some steps," she said.

After a while she came up her steps, groaning. With her waist above ground, she glared at Kalle and demanded crossly, "Well, now what? Am I supposed to fly?"

"I don't know," said Kalle.

Oma tried to fly. She jumped up, clung to the edge of the pit, wriggled one leg like a frog, and hauled herself up inch by inch. Kalle had to laugh. First Oma was kneeling on the edge, then she stood up, then she brushed off her skirt, then she hit Kalle. "Laugh, will you?" she said. "That's it! This is the last vacation I'm going on. Ever!"

When they were sitting in the living room that evening, however, Oma told the story of the turnip pit very differently from the way it happened. She made it a lot more exciting. Especially when she told how she got out. According to Oma, she got out in one single leap.

"Just imagine an old woman like me still being able to jump like that!" she said.

Kalle was angry to hear her lying.

That night, when he woke up, Oma asked him why he wasn't asleep. He could have said, "Because my nose is stuffy," but what he said was: "Because you lied."

Oma laughed. Then she said, "I'll tell you something. When you've had as dull a life as I have, you have to invent some excitement. Don't you think so?"

Kalle didn't think so.

It did turn out to be the only time they went on vacation together. As time went on, Oma made up even more stories about their vacation—amazing adventures. Kalle got used to having taken part in things that had never happened outside Oma's head. He also stopped pointing out that she was telling lies. If Oma couldn't go on vacation, she needed her stories.

Well, am I Frau Erna Bittel or am I some nobody they can do with as they please! No, I'm never going to travel like that again, not if Kalle was to stand on his head and beg me! I'm not used to that kind of treatment. I had to work hard and I got along with people. Strange faces make me twitch. Still, the boy ought to see a bit of the world. I'll think of something. If you ask me, I'll take our street here in Munich over any fancy vacation in the Bavarian Forest. Even if I can't keep up with young Kalle! He'd better go to camp the next time, so he can have plenty of exercise and adventures and good country air.

7

The Social Worker
Visits Oma and Kalle

Kalle was in his third year at school now. Things weren't going very well. Oma tried to help him with his homework, but at times she got stuck herself and exclaimed, "This stupid stuff gives me a headache! Why do they make you poor little things work so hard?"

Kalle wondered too. He decided to give Oma (and himself) less homework, by doing only about half of it. His teacher, Frau Riemer, put up with this for a while. She only scolded him a little. But after three weeks she gave him a letter to take home to Oma. Kalle threw it down a drain. But that evening his conscience bothered him so much that he confessed. "Oma, I threw away a letter for you today."

Oma asked who had written the letter.

"Frau Riemer," said Kalle.

"Do you know what was in it?" Oma asked.

"No," said Kalle.

"Then you must ask Frau Riemer tomorrow," Oma told him.

Kalle got scared and started to cry.

"All right, I'll go and see her," said Oma.

"But she doesn't have consulting hours tomorrow," said Kalle.

"I don't care," said Oma. "I have to know what was in the letter, right?"

Oma arrived in the middle of a lesson. The door opened and there was Oma. Kalle felt like crawling under his desk. His friends snickered. Oma stood there looking serious. Frau Riemer was surprised. She asked Oma why she was here.

"It's about that letter," said Oma.

"Yes, that's terrible, isn't it?" said Frau Riemer.

"I agree," said Oma.

"We'll have to get some help," said Frau Riemer.

"What for?" asked Oma.

"But didn't you understand my letter?" asked Frau Riemer.

"I haven't read it," said Oma.

"How come you are here about my letter if you haven't read it?" Frau Riemer sounded puzzled.

"Because I don't have it anymore."

"Didn't Kalle give it to you?"

"It's gone. Disappeared. I put it down and can't remember where," said Oma. And Kalle loved her.

Frau Riemer left the room with Oma and came

back a few minutes later. She patted Kalle's head. "Everything's going to be all right," she said.

Kalle could hardly wait to hear what Frau Riemer had said to Oma. Oma snorted.

"You aren't doing your homework, only half, that is. And you keep getting it wrong," she said crossly.

"But *you* can't do it either," said Kalle.

"I'm not a schoolchild, am I?" said Oma.

"But you're old, Oma, you must know everything!" said Kalle.

"There's an awful lot I've forgotten," she said.

They discussed how to get Kalle's homework done without too many mistakes. Oma sighed and said she'd just have to study with him from his books.

It may have been the letter that brought the social worker to Oma's apartment. Or perhaps the school had notified the welfare department, because the principal and Kalle's teacher knew the department was responsible for him as an orphan. Maybe the welfare department simply wanted to see how Kalle did his homework, if he had a quiet place where he could do it, and whether Oma could help him if necessary.

In any case, the social worker came. She was very pretty, with thick green eye shadow. Kalle liked her. Oma did not. She would have liked to toss her out the window. The social worker sat at the table in their living room-kitchen, with Oma standing in front of her and Kalle curled up in a corner of the sofa. She asked questions endlessly. Why had Oma taken Kalle in after his parents' death, did he have any younger relatives, had Oma had any infectious diseases, did she go to the doctor a lot, did Kalle have any reading difficulties, did he have a room of his own?

Oma, grinding her false teeth, gave her a tour of the apartment, pointed to Kalle's bed, and said, "Soft and clean, right?" She lifted the lid off the pan on the stove. "And the boy gets fed properly too," she said.

The social worker kept nodding.

At last Oma couldn't restrain herself any longer. She pushed the social worker back into her chair and, her hands on the woman's shoulders, breathed into her face and said very softly, "Well, young lady, what are you really after? Am I an old witch out of a fairy tale? Am I senile? Have I lost the use of my limbs? Have I been running around the streets stark naked? Has Kalle been stealing things? Or what?"

The social worker tried to smile, and answered in an equally soft voice, "No, none of those things, Frau Bittel. It's just that the school is worried about Kalle, because he isn't doing his homework properly. So we wondered . . ."

"You wondered what?" asked Oma threateningly.

"Well, whether your affairs were . . ."

"What affairs?"

52

"I mean, whether you were really in a position to . . ."

Oma was shouting now: "Affairs, indeed! At my age! How dare you!"

Kalle tried to sneak out of the room, but Oma grabbed him and said, "You stay put! I want you to hear this. I need a witness!"

Ever since Oma had started visiting the Powers That Be, she had been very big on having witnesses. "It's very important if you don't want them to cheat you," she'd say.

The social worker was so intimidated she stopped talking about Oma's affairs, and instead said she thought everything was fine, but she'd like to pay a visit every two months, and to help if need be. Oma became friendly again, but she said, "No one's helped me up to now, young lady, and it's too late to start now! We're over the worst of it, Kalle and I."

Then the social worker said something that really scared Kalle. "Still, something might happen to you someday. Or you could be sick and have to go to the hospital. What would happen to the child then?"

"I won't be sick!" said Oma, pushing her out of the door.

She won't be sick, Kalle told himself whenever he imagined Oma being taken off in an ambulance, even dying. She won't be sick.

Maybe I've gone wrong with Kalle somewhere. That business with the letter. Am I too soft? But what does soft mean? I'd rather reason with him than shout at him. Anyway, shouting's so exhausting. All right, I'm soft on him because I love him. . . . Well, they say love is the best thing for a child, don't they? And now it's not enough anymore? He's telling lies, doing badly in school, is he? Nonsense, I'll talk to him, give him a hard time and tell him he needn't be scared of the welfare office and the social worker and all that. I can't see anything wrong with me and Kalle. Now I'm exaggerating. I know. Still, it helps.

8

Oma Is Scared

It wasn't that Oma drank too much. She didn't. But she did keep a bottle of brandy in her glass-fronted cupboard, and Kalle could see the level going down a little each day. When he first mentioned it to Oma she was mad.

"I won't tolerate spying, Kalle. Drinking, indeed! What does that mean? One little nip a day." Then she mumbled, "Or a couple of nips twice a day."

Kalle didn't mean to suggest that she drank. He had never seen her drunk, like some of the men who lived in their building, or old Frau Lederer on the top floor. He only wondered why she kept it a secret from him. "Why do you hide the bottle?" he asked.

Oma sat down on the sofa. She made Kalle sit down too, though he didn't want to, but he hoped she was going to tell a story about the old days that he hadn't heard before.

It did begin like a story. "Your grandpa sometimes

drank too much, Kalle. To tell the truth, sometimes he came home reeling, and I swore I'd never touch the stuff myself. Even when we were invited out, or when we celebrated something, I hardly took a drop. Well, I do now, and do you know why? It's simple, really. The day your grandfather died I was so restless, I kept running around the apartment trying to tidy it up, but only making a mess. Then I found two bottles in Grandpa's bedside cabinet. Suddenly I felt furious with him, even though I was so unhappy. I unscrewed the top of one and took a big swig—it was like showing poor dead Grandpa how angry I was! And you know something, Kalle? It did me good. I said to myself, 'This really warms the soul!' And since then I've warmed my soul with a glass or two. Especially when I feel scared."

Kalle looked at her in surprise. "But you're never scared, Oma! I've never seen such a thing."

"Well, you're eight now, Kalle, and you know quite a lot, but you can't always *see* fear."

Kalle insisted that he *would* know if she was scared. Oma laughed. "Very sure of yourself, aren't you? I'm not scared of that fat man at the welfare office, of or the social worker, or the superintendent here, or anyone at all. I'm scared of something quite different. Well, not one thing. Lots of things.

"I'm scared there'll be another inflation and my savings will go up in smoke. I wasn't much more than a child in 1923, and my father, that's your great-grandfather, hadn't been able to save much. But all of a sudden the little bit he *had* saved wasn't worth anything. Something that used to cost one mark suddenly cost thousands of marks. It was crazy! And then in 1931, when money meant something again, there wasn't any work. I was newly married; your grandfather had lost his job and had to go on welfare, and that wasn't much. We hardly knew how to make ends meet.

"That's what I'm scared of. And I'm scared I'll get sick. What will become of you then? Every time you go to school, I'm scared something will happen to you. I'm scared they'll raise our rent. Those are the kinds of things that scare me, and I can't shake off my fears. Every day I talk myself into them, and then try and talk myself out of them. When things get to be too much, I go to that cupboard and pour myself a little drink, drink it down, and tell myself, 'Come on, Erna, you're not scared!' And it works for a while."

Kalle could understand that.

He's discovered I take a drop now and then. Probably thinks I'm an old soak! I tried to explain. Funny how silly I feel, explaining things like that. How can the boy understand what scares me? Or maybe he does understand—just a little. Perhaps he knows me better than I think. If so, it's all right. A little nip now and then— well, I need it.

9

Oma Likes Soccer

Kalle might not be brilliant in all subjects at school, and he did not always do his homework, but he was popular with the other boys. He had lots of ideas for games, was always ready to join in things, he was a good fighter, and above all he was an excellent soccer player. His friend Martin, a tall, thin boy whose hobby was astronomy, was the best goalkeeper of his grade. It was Martin's idea to organize a third-grade soccer team, which he was sure would beat the fourth-grade boys.

Kalle was center forward. They knew what a center forward was from radio and television. He was clearly the player who really made the game.

For a while the team trained during recess. Then the teachers heard about it and suggested they meet in the park after school. One of the teachers would come along.

Kalle thought that was a terrific idea. He told Oma

the moment he got home, but she was against it. She said he might break his leg playing such a rough game, or someone might knock a hole in his head. She said, "No, it won't do, Kalle! I'm easy-going— but you aren't even properly supervised!"

"We don't *need* anyone to keep an eye on us!" said Kalle. "You always want me to have a nursemaid or something! Come on, please let me go! Our first training session is Thursday."

Oma could never hold out against Kalle for long. She asked him where they were playing.

"It's not far from here," said Kalle. "In the park—you know, close to where people play tennis."

"Yes, I know," said Oma. "People with nothing better to do."

"Don't be silly, Oma," said Kalle. "If you could play tennis you'd go there too!"

"You know how much a little white dress like that costs?" asked Oma.

"I couldn't care less," said Kalle.

"Neither could I!" said Oma. "But that's why I can't play tennis."

So on Thursday Kalle went to the park with the ball, which he had been keeping at home. It was a black-and-white ball; even Oma thought it was pretty.

One of the young teachers from school was there. He taught the boys a lot. How to trap the ball with your chest or your feet, how to kick it with the side of your foot or with your toes. Kalle liked heading the ball best. That's what he was best at. Martin moved around in the goal like a snake—leaping into the air, falling flat in the mud, anything to keep the ball out.

They were in the middle of the match when, to his horror, Kalle saw Oma standing at the edge of the field. She waved to him. He paid no attention; he was terribly embarrassed. After a while she started shouting. At first Kalle, who was not looking at her, thought she was mad at him. Then he heard her egging him or the other boys on. He heard her shout, "Faster, Kalle! Look out for that fat boy! That wasn't fair! Come on, don't let them get that ball away from you!"

The teacher went over to her, and they talked for a while. Kalle watched them out of the corner of his eye. The teacher kept laughing. Oma must be telling him lots of funny stories.

She stayed until the end of the game. She even applauded. Not that she had understood much of it, which was probably why the teacher laughed so much. She used all the wrong soccer expressions, and Kalle didn't feel like explaining everything. She'd never really understand the game, he thought. But after that she didn't grumble whenever he went out to play soccer.

He did hurt himself in one of their next matches.

He had been clumsy. He had stumbled and sprained his ankle. He hadn't even had the ball at the time! The ankle swelled up, and Kalle couldn't stand on it.

The teacher took him home in his car.

To Kalle's surprise, Oma didn't make a fuss. She stayed quite calm, thanked the teacher, examined the ankle, and said, "Nothing broken!" She didn't even call the doctor, though Kalle said it hurt badly.

"Yes, I know," she said. "But I'll put compresses on it and the pain will soon be gone. Only you'll have to keep your foot up for a few days."

Oma was marvelous. She didn't go out on her rounds with the leaflets; she stayed at home with him, moved the television so that he could see it from his bed, and played Parcheesi and tiddlywinks with him. When he started to get bored on the third day, she offered to teach him to knit. But he refused.

Kalle was afraid Oma wouldn't let him play soccer anymore, but he was wrong. The first day back at school she even asked, "Is there a match today?"

"Not till tomorrow," Kalle told her.

"You'll have to be careful of your leg, of course," she said, "but be sure to play well, Kalle!"

If Kalle only knew how I pretend to him sometimes! Take that soccer business. I was terribly worried. I thought Kalle was fibbing to me, just wanted to loaf around, that there wasn't any soccer or helpful teacher at all. Did I feel ashamed for not trusting him! Erna Bittel, you must never do a thing like that again!

IO

Why Kalle Sometimes
Fights with Oma

Now and then Kalle and Oma had a fight: when she
wouldn't let him go to see the new Western, when
she didn't like one of his friends, or when she made
Kalle put on his warmer jacket even though the sun
was shining. But those are just ordinary everyday
arguments. The only real quarrels they had were
about Kalle's mother. Of course, Kalle couldn't really
remember her clearly now, but he still had the feeling
she was very close to him, the person he loved most.
Oma, however, loved her son, Kalle's father, more.
Years after Kalle's mother died, Oma was still finding
fault with her. She thought her daughter-in-law had
made a number of mistakes—in the way she brought
Kalle up, among other things.

As soon as Oma started on this subject, Kalle
would feel a surge of hot anger rise inside him. He'd
jump to his mother's defense. "It's none of your

business!" he shouted. "Anyway, how do *you* know what Mommy was like?"

"I know better than you do!" said Oma.

So the fight would begin. Kalle wasn't sure why Oma provoked him like that. She shouldn't; she shouldn't talk about his mother at all, Kalle felt. Sometimes Oma seemed to get really worked up over her memories of Kalle's mother. He couldn't see why.

"You weren't enemies or anything," he said. "She was my mother, wasn't she? Your son's wife?"

"Indeed she was," said Oma, but she made it sound nasty.

Kalle usually cried when they had these arguments. Once he attacked Oma, hitting her with his clenched fists. Oma didn't forgive him for days. She obviously didn't understand that he still loved his mother as much as if she were alive, or even more. Maybe she was jealous of his mother. That could be it.

"If you only knew how horrible she could be to me sometimes!" said Oma.

"Oh, come on, Oma! You don't know how nice Mommy was, you just have no idea!" cried Kalle.

"Nice to you, maybe," Oma retorted.

"Well, she didn't have to be nice to you," shouted Kalle. "I bet you were horrible to her, too! You weren't important!"

"Oh, and now?" Oma said triumphantly. "Am I unimportant now?"

"Oh, leave me alone!" Kalle sobbed. He couldn't make himself admit that she was just as important to him now as his mother used to be.

All right, so I never particularly liked my daughter-in-law, and I can see the boy still thinks a lot of her. I'm his grandmother and I'm alive. She was his mother and she's dead. She was no saint, I can tell you, but he's making her into one! Is that any reason I should never breathe a word again her? Funny thing . . . he really provokes me with his "Mommy used to do this . . ." "Mommy didn't do that. . . ." Yes, well, I'm the one here now! Death doesn't make a person any better than she was, but I must try not to annoy him, I really must. It isn't easy.

II

Oma Wins a Prize

Oma entered almost every contest she saw in the papers or magazines. Kalle had caught the bug from her. They often sent in their entries together. Kalle actually won something once: a bright yellow crash helmet, much too big for him. He kept it on a hook in his room. Oma was angry when the parcel with the crash helmet came. "You've just started and you've won a prize already!" she said. "Look at me—I've been entering contests for years, and I never won a thing!"

Kalle tried to cheer her up. "I bet you'll win first prize someday," he said.

And she did. At first she didn't know which contest it was in, because she had sent in entries for at least twelve. The first news of her prize came in a telegram. It said: "Congratulations! You have won a plane ticket for a circle trip over Munich!"

"What's that supposed to mean?" Oma asked Kalle.

"It means you go up in a plane and fly all over the city in a big circle!"

"But I don't want to," said Oma. "I want to have a substitute prize!"

"Why not wait and see what happens?" Kalle suggested.

After the telegram they didn't hear any more for days. Oma, who was scared stiff of her prize, could think of nothing else. She ran to the door every time the bell rang, only to be disappointed when it was a neighbor or the mailman with no more news of the prize.

"*I* think they were pulling my leg," she said.

"You can't expect them to be that quick," Kalle told her. "They need time to buy your plane ticket."

"But I don't want any plane ticket," said Oma.

"Well, they can't know that, can they?" said Kalle.

"Nonsense!" Oma got cross every time she mentioned her prize. "They must know an old woman like me wouldn't want to go up in a plane!"

They were having supper. Kalle laughed. Oma snapped at him not to lounge in his chair like that, and not to put his elbows on the table. "Listen," Kalle said, "what makes you think they know you're an old woman? Did you have to give your age or something?"

Oma started to think, but Kalle went on, "I bet you didn't! You never have to give your age unless there's some reason you can't sign on your own behalf, and even then you don't always have to give it, and you *can* sign for yourself, can't you?"

"Of course! What do you think I am—mentally deficient?"

"No—what's that got to do with it?"

On his way to school the next day Kalle was wondering what he could do. He decided to write to the company that was giving her the prize. That afternoon, while Oma was out distributing leaflets, he wrote a letter:

Dear Contest Organizer,

I am Frau Erna Bittel's grandson; she won the flight over Munich in your contest but there's something she doesn't dare tell you so I am going to. She doesn't want the prize. She doesn't want to go up in a plane. She's scared. You see, my grandmother hasn't ever flown before. I haven't either. I wish you could give my grandmother something Omas like. Then she would be happy.

Sincerely yours,
Kalle Bittel

Kalle found a stamp, stuck it on the envelope, and mailed the letter before Oma got home. He hoped something would happen soon now. He was disappointed: Nothing happened, and Oma got more and more nervous. But at last, three weeks later, there was a letter from the company. It was not addressed to Oma but to Kalle, which upset Oma. Kalle was at school when it came, and she couldn't open it. She wouldn't. She had promised Kalle never to open his mail and said he must never open hers. It wasn't right. She was like a cat on hot coals, telling herself it wouldn't be right to open Kalle's letter. And he would be at school for six whole hours! Oma almost went crazy with curiosity. She held the letter up to the light, but there was no writing visible through the envelope. She wondered whether to steam it open, but then she thought that would be cheating Kalle. So she waited. To make waiting easier she went to the baker's, bought a small loaf, and stopped for a long chat, until finally the baker said, "Frau Bittel, I really have to go to the back now."

She knew she shouldn't have kept him talking so long, but what else could she do? At long last she heard Kalle outside the door of the apartment, and she ran to open it, calling out, "Kalle, you've got a letter! It's from the people giving me my plane flight!"

Kalle just nodded and walked past her into his room.

"Aren't you even interested?" screamed Oma.

"Coming. I have to put my school things away first," said Kalle.

"You can do that later!" cried Oma.

"Then you'll start in at me about being untidy."

"No, I won't."

"Yes, you will. You always do."

"Not today!"

Kalle was taking his time, while Oma paced feverishly up and down the kitchen. "God, what a horrible child!" she groaned.

She brought him a knife to help open the envelope. Kalle unfolded the letter maddeningly slowly, and held it so that Oma couldn't read it. As he read he nodded, began to grin, and then folded the letter up again.

"Well, what is it?" Oma asked.

"Everything's fixed," said Kalle.

"What do you mean? Why are they writing to you, anyway? *I* won the prize, not you!" cried Oma.

"But you didn't want it," said Kalle.

"Well, they couldn't know that," said Oma.

"That's right," said Kalle. He felt terribly clever. "So I wrote to them."

"You? Are you crazy? Interfering in my business

73

affairs!" shouted Oma. "Ruining them all!"

Kalle was cooler than ever. "I haven't ruined anything, Oma," he said. "I've only straightened things out."

"Well, go on!"

"*I'm* going to have the plane ride," said Kalle. "They've transferred the prize to me, because you're too old."

Oma sat down on the kitchen stool, the way she always did when she was too angry or excited to stand, and stared at him wide-eyed.

"You stole my prize! My only grandson, stealing from me, writing letters behind my back! I call it shocking! I'm going to complain to the welfare department!" she said.

"If you do I'll never speak to you again!" said Kalle. "And I won't tell you what else the letter says, either."

"Well, what does it say?"

"You're getting a substitute prize."

"Never!"

"Yes, they're inviting you to dinner in the airport restaurant while I'm up in the air—a really posh meal!"

"Fobbing me off like that!" said Oma. But actually she liked the idea: They didn't lose the plane trip, and she didn't mind a good dinner, except that she'd be scared to think of Kalle up in that plane.

"But from now on my business correspondence has nothing to do with you!" said Oma. "This is the last time you ever stick *your* nose into it!"

There I go again, getting so angry with the boy for being independent when really I ought to be thankful! So what if he sticks his nose into my affairs now and then? I acted pretty helpless myself, didn't I? I ought to encourage Kalle to be independent, that's what.

12

The Old-Folks' Home

"I promised Frau Wendelin months ago to visit her one Sunday," Oma said. "And you're coming with me," she told Kalle. "I'll never survive all those old people without you."

"Where does Frau Wendelin live?" asked Kalle.

"In the old-folks' home at Obermenzing," Oma told him.

"I don't want to go," said Kalle.

"But you will." Oma refused to listen to any objections. She put on her strange Sunday outfit, which she only wore on special occasions like trips and going to visit the Powers That Be, and told Kalle to put on his own best clothes; and they took the tram to Obermenzing.

There were obviously a great many old people living in the big building they went into; even the garden around it seemed full of them.

Oma could see that Kalle felt uncomfortable. "You

think you'll be young forever, do you?" she said roughly.

"No, but I won't be *that* old!" said Kalle. "If I do grow old I'll be like you."

Oma laughed. "Kalle, if you didn't know me—if you were visiting this place with someone else—you'd think I was just another of the old people living here."

Kalle said no more.

They met Frau Wendelin in a big room which felt remarkably uncomfortable, full of round tables and old armchairs. Frau Wendelin was a tiny little old lady whose head kept waggling slightly. Oma seemed really glad to see her. She introduced Kalle. "This is my grandson," she said proudly. "He lives with me, you know."

It was much too hot in the room, which smelled musty and airless. Kalle was sweating. He took off his jacket. He noticed that Oma was hot too, because after a while she took her hat off. He didn't really listen to the conversation between the two old women. Oma was talking about him a lot, while Frau Wendelin went on about her only son, a pilot who had been lost in the war—"In the flower of his youth," she kept saying. "In the flower of his youth."

Kalle watched the other old people sitting around the tables. Most of them seemed quite normal, but some were smiling or grinning to themselves in a

funny way, or talking out loud to no one. A nurse was helping some of them with their food. Others sat in their chairs without moving, as if they were already dead. Kalle was not exactly afraid of them, but it was a depressing place. A world that had nothing to do with him.

He and Oma were silent for much of the way home. Finally Oma said, "It's a dreadful thing, living all huddled together like that. All so old, so terribly old!"

Kalle found it difficult to put what he wanted to say into words. "I know you're old too, Oma—but not like that. They're different."

"They're not, you know," said Oma. "I'm as old as they are. Only I'm on my own—and I spend my time with you, and you're young. That makes a difference. Old age is dreadful if there are so many other old people around that you can't see life going on around you, that's all. But the world is frightened of old age. You are too, Kalle."

Kalle remembered the heat and the stuffiness and the closed-in feeling that had oppressed him. He thought Oma was right. He thought Oma was terrific.

Just as well for Kalle to see what it's like, all those old people crammed together in a home.

I didn't want to go myself; I'd much rather not have gone. I don't think I'm that old either!

That's Kalle's doing, of course. If I didn't have Kalle to look after I daresay I could dwell on every little pain I get and moan and groan and get on people's nerves! You could say Kalle was my medicine, in a way.

13

Oma Talks Back
to the Television

At first Kalle and Oma used to argue about who watched what on television. In time the problem solved itself, because Oma didn't care that much for television. She preferred to read the paper or sew. Anyway, she thought the Westerns or crime shows Kalle liked were boring. But she insisted on watching old movies she'd already seen, and if one was being shown it was no use for Kalle to want a different program. She would usually send him to bed, saying, "You wouldn't understand this. You're too young. It was all so long ago."

Kalle did watch half of one film with her; he thought it was soppy and boring, but Oma wept and wept.

One night Kalle woke up and heard Oma talking. He was startled because she hadn't said anything about expecting guests. He crept to the door, opened it very quietly, and peered into the room. Oma was by herself, sitting in front of the television set and talking to it. She was very upset.

"Bilge, absolute bilge!" she cried. Kalle memorized the word and decided to ask Oma what it meant.

"Sheer bilge!" she went on. "Nobody lives that way, not even rich people! I don't know why they think this stuff up. Just to make fools of us, I suppose. This has nothing to do with real people. Things like that don't happen. Why, look at me and Kalle, and my pension and Kalle's allowance. They never show you that kind of thing, do they? Oh no! I don't know why I'm watching, I really don't!"

Kalle shut the door again quietly, because he had to laugh. Oma was so funny when she was mad. The next morning he asked her, "Oma, what's bilge?"

Oma put down her cup in surprise. "Why?" she asked.

Kalle was a little embarrassed. "Well, you were watching television last night and you kept shouting at it and saying it was all bilge!"

"Oh," said Oma. "Well, it means something's garbage, nonsense, not worth anything."

"What kind of movie were you watching, Oma?" Kalle asked.

"What they call a problem play or something. About some highfalutin people in England or America—crazy, the whole lot of them, never do a stroke of work but all the same they're crazy and miserable, or they act that way. God knows why!"

"But that sounds funny!" said Kalle. "The sort of movies you like are all full of people running around in old-fashioned clothes crying and kissing each other and so on."

"You don't understand," said Oma. "Life was like that in the old days."

"I don't believe it!" said Kalle. "Like in that movie where the girl was lying on the rooftop and she nearly fell off? I've never seen anyone do that!"

"Oh, but that was all because of the inheritance," said Oma.

"What's inheritance?"

"When someone dies, other people—usually relatives—get the dead person's money and houses and factories and so on," Oma tried to explain.

"Well, *you* don't have much money, or any houses or factories," said Kalle.

"No, but these people in the film had masses of money, and they wanted to get the inheritance away from the girl, who should have gotten it, and that was disgusting."

"Who cares?" said Kalle. "I think those films are boring."

"I think Westerns are boring. And they're not true either. Did you ever see anyone ride through town shooting?" asked Oma.

"No, but they do in America," said Kalle.

"All the same . . ." said Oma, looking for a fight. Kalle didn't feel like fighting, so he changed the subject. "I think bilge is a marvelous word," he said.

It's good to know what bilge is. But the way Kalle makes fun of me watching tearjerkers— no, really! I shouldn't put up with it. He wasn't so far wrong, though; some of those old films were real weepies. As for these newfangled programs, I just don't understand them. Maybe I ought to discuss politics with Kalle. My Otto would never talk politics. He always said, "I'm not joining any party, I'm not getting mixed up in any dirty business like politics." Even though he didn't have much in life. He could have fought for his rights, couldn't he? I remember how Otto yelled at me when I joined the Social Democratic party after the war. I don't think Otto was right to do that. I don't want Kalle not standing up for his beliefs.

14

Oma Gets Sick

Kalle could never really imagine that Oma might get sick. For a long time she didn't, but just before his tenth birthday the thing he had secretly half feared happened. Oma tried to hide it for several days. She stayed in bed later than usual, asked Kalle to get his own breakfast, sent him to the baker's for her, and distributed hardly any leaflets. In fact she did all sorts of unusual things.

"Don't you feel well?" asked Kalle.

"Oh, I'm fine," said Oma. "Just a little tired. It's the spring weather." It was not. On the fifth or sixth day Oma said she thought she had a temperature, and she'd have to call the doctor.

Kalle was very upset, though he tried not to show it. "Would you like me to go for the doctor?" he asked.

"Yes, do that," said Oma.

Kalle rang the doctor's doorbell. According to the

sign by the door it wasn't office hours, and the young woman who opened it was rather brusque. "Can't you come at the proper time?" she asked.

"My grandmother's sick," he said.

The doctor's receptionist looked at him and shook her head. "Frau Bittel? Never!"

"She really *is* sick. She has a temperature, and if Oma says she needs the doctor, then . . ." Kalle was near tears.

"Dr. Hinz will come right away, Kalle, don't you worry!" Now the receptionist was nice to him.

"Good," said Kalle, "but *really* right away, please!"

"As soon as he comes back from his rounds," the receptionist promised.

And the doctor did come. He sent Kalle out of the room because he had to give Oma a thorough examination.

Kalle sat in his room and didn't know what to do with himself. He thought of the little speech Oma had made on his last birthday, imagined what would happen if she died, mumbled to himself, "Oma mustn't die." He felt like a five-year-old.

There was a knock at the door; the doctor wanted him. They sat by Oma's bed, and the doctor said, "Now, Kalle, listen to me. You mustn't worry. Oma has had a nasty attack of angina, but she's in good shape for her age. Right, Frau Bittel?"

Oma beamed and nodded.

"Now, I don't think it's a good idea for Oma to be here with no one to nurse her," the doctor went on. "It's not a job you could do, Kalle. So I want her to spend a week in the hospital. We've talked it over. I'm going to ask the woman next door to look in on you, and I'll also let the social worker know."

"No, not her!" said Kalle.

"Yes, her too," said the doctor firmly. "We must have everything shipshape, or your grandmother will worry and then she won't get better quickly."

"Oh, all right," said Kalle.

"An ambulance will come for Oma tomorrow morning. You should take the day off from school. I'll write you a note."

"OK," said Kalle, and he found he was growing very calm. Now that things were serious, he had to show them Oma could rely on him.

Oma was taken away very early the next morning. After Kalle had shut the door of the apartment again he began to cry. It was so early he could still have gone to school, but he didn't. He began to straighten the place up, the way Oma always did. Later the bell rang and it was the woman from next door to ask when he would like his lunch.

"Not yet," said Kalle.

"Goodness, everything's shiny in here!" she said. He was pleased. In the afternoon he went to play soccer. At five he went to see Oma at the hospital. He was going to go every day, though visiting times were only supposed to be three days a week. He had special permission.

Oma looked tired and asked only a few questions. Kalle sat beside her and didn't know what to say. He should have thought of something to talk about beforehand.

The social worker visited him after school the next day, when he was eating his lunch. She was new. "I'm Fräulein Hauschild," she introduced herself.

"I'm Kalle Bittel," said Kalle.

She laughed. "Yes, I know," she said. "Is there anything I can do to help?"

"Not really," he said. "I'm all right."

"Fine," she said. "Still, I'll look in once a day anyway, and if anything's bothering you, just let me know. The woman next door is giving you your meals, isn't she?"

"Yes," said Kalle.

"And you don't *have* to keep the place so incredibly clean!" she said.

Kalle liked her.

When he went to see Oma the next day, the nurse wouldn't let him in. Oma was still rather weak, she said, and she mustn't get excited.

Kalle was scared. The awful, unthinkable thing was going to happen. He must try and be ready for it.

"Oma's dying," he told Fräulein Hauschild. "I know she is."

"Nonsense, Kalle," said Fräulein Hauschild. "I just called to find out how she's doing."

"She is, though," said Kalle, "and I'll have to go into an orphanage."

"No, no," said Fräulein Hauschild, but he could see she didn't want to discuss it any further.

Fräulein Hauschild came every day, late in the afternoon. Sometimes she watched television with him, or she had a look at his homework, or talked to the woman next door. She was really nice. She didn't ask a lot of questions. She just made sure nothing went wrong.

A few days later he could visit Oma again. Once or twice Fräulein Hauschild took him to the hospital. Oma was recovering quickly now. He didn't have to rack his brain for things to say anymore, because Oma was telling stories again, asking questions, telling him what to do.

She came home after exactly two weeks. Kalle had cleaned the apartment and stuck a piece of paper to the front door, saying WELCOME HOME! in red crayon.

Oma came home in style, by taxi. Kalle could hear her laughing outside the door. So she liked his sign! This time it wasn't Oma who hugged him—*he* hugged *her,* for the first time ever. She went all over the apartment, looking at everything, and said he'd done a marvelous job. "Well, we're back in business, Kalle," she said, giving him a nudge.

She was just going to make coffee when the bell rang, and it was the woman next door with a bunch of flowers. Oma thanked her, the bell rang again, and it was the baker's wife with a cake. Oma was telling them all about her illness, in great detail, when there was still another ring, and it was Fräulein Hauschild. All of a sudden they were all sitting around the table, Kalle among them, everyone very happy and saying Oma looked wonderful, as if she'd had a real rest.

"Rest! I like that!" said Oma.

That evening, after the party, she decided to go to bed earlier than usual. "I must take it easy in the evenings," she said.

"It's terrible without you, Oma," said Kalle.

"You see!" she said. "But you must learn to do without me, you know."

Kalle knew she was right. He remembered how scared he had been, but then he thought of all the people who had helped him. He mustn't always rely on other people.

He heard Oma turn the key in her bedroom door and get undressed, groaning slightly, just the same as usual. Surely nothing would change just yet!

"Good night, Oma," he called.

"Sleep well, Kalle," she replied. "I'll wake you in the morning."

"OK, Oma." He didn't have to set the alarm. Oma was back in charge.

Well, I thought, this is the end of you, Erna Bittel! When the boy went to get Dr. Hinz so many things went through my head. What would happen to him afterward, would anyone take him to live with them, or would he have to go into an orphanage? I wanted to get up so no one would notice anything, but I felt so dreadful, I thought I was going to die.

That's over. We are back together. I think Kalle has become more attentive—more thoughtful, somehow. I daresay it gave him quite a shock. Of course it would be better if he still had his parents, better for him anyway. Not for me, no, not for me! Maybe I can't do much at times, but Kalle means a second lease on life for me. I hope to have a few more years!

15

Kalle Turns Ten

When Kalle turned ten all his friends were invited to a birthday party. Oma behaved beautifully: She wasn't cross once, she put up with the noise and even joined in games. And she didn't say a thing when one of the boys spilled juice on the carpet.

It was on Kalle's tenth birthday that Oma explained to him why things wouldn't go on like this forever.

The boys had gone home, and Kalle was out of breath. He was wearing the great training suit Oma had given him. She asked him to sit beside her on the sofa and made a little speech—without looking at him, though she held his hand lightly in hers.

"Well, you're ten now, Kalle," she said, "and I believe a person of ten can face facts and think. And you have a lot behind you. I can expect you to think seriously, can't I? I'm over seventy. I know I don't look it, but that's sixty years older than you. Can you picture that much time?"

Kalle, alarmed, said, "No."

"I thought not," said Oma. "Now, it's important for you to think about it. I won't live to be a hundred. And that illness I had . . .

"Well, let's assume I have eight years left. Eight years is quite a lot. Then you'd be eighteen, and independent. But suppose I have only four years left . . ."

"I don't believe it!" Kalle interrupted.

"Well, I'm glad of that. *I* don't believe it either, but you must face the possibility, see? There's that aunt of yours in Bottrop, I forget her name. Your mother's sister. She's never bothered about you, but she might take you in. Otherwise you'd have to go to an orphanage, Kalle."

"No!" said Kalle firmly.

"You'd have to, there wouldn't be any alternative," said Oma.

"Then I'd run away," said Kalle.

"That's stupid," said Oma. "Some orphanages are nice."

Hesitantly, Kalle asked, "Do you think you're going to die soon, Oma?"

"I've made up my mind to live as long as I possibly can, Kalle," said Oma. "But making up your mind isn't enough, though it helps."

She hugged him, something she seldom did now. She smelled of cooking and old clothes. Kalle almost cried, because he was scared and because he realized he didn't know very much about her, but that he loved her very much.

"We'll do our best," said Oma. "But I've explained things to you. And that's important."

Format by Kohar Alexanian
Set in 13 pt. Avanta
Composed and bound by The Haddon Craftsmen,
Scranton, Penna.
Printed by The Murray Printing Company
HARPER & ROW, PUBLISHERS, INC.

D/T